WHO WAS BORN THIS SPECIAL DAY?

Eve Bunting

∿: *and* :∿

Leonid Gore

ALADDIN PAPERBACKS

NEW YORK   LONDON   TORONTO   SYDNEY   SINGAPORE

First Aladdin Paperbacks edition October 2003

Text copyright © 2000 by Eve Bunting
Illustrations copyright © 2000 by Leonid Gore

ALADDIN PAPERBACKS
An imprint of Simon & Schuster
Children's Publishing Division
1230 Avenue of the Americas
New York, NY 10020

Also available in an Atheneum Books for Young Readers hardcover edition.
Designed by Angela Carlino
The text of this book was set in Vendetta Medium.
The illustrations were rendered in acrylic paint on paper.

Manufactured in China
2 4 6 8 10 9 7 5 3 1

The Library of Congress has cataloged the hardcover edition as follows:
Bunting, Eve, 1928–
Who was born this special day? / by Eve Bunting; illustrations by Leonid Gore.
p. cm.
Summary: Not the lamb nor the goat nor the donkey nor the dove was born on the first
Christmas long ago, but a special child was.
ISBN 0-689-82302-9 (hc.)
1. Jesus Christ—Juvenile poetry. 2. Children's poetry, American. 3. Christian poetry,
American. [1. Jesus Christ—Nativity poetry. 2. American poetry.] I. Gore, Leonid, ill.
II. Title.
PS3552.U4735W48   2000 811'.54—dc21   99-27675

ISBN 0-689-85955-4 (Aladdin pbk.)

To my daughter Christine
—E. B.

For Harriet, with appreciation
—L. G.

*W*ho was born this special day?

Was it you, little lamb?

"I was born back in early May
when the breezes of spring chased winter away."

It was not the lamb.

Was it you, little goat?

"No, not I.
I was born on a soft, warm night
under the white of the moon's pale light."

It was not the goat.

Who was born this special day?
Was it you, little calf?

"I breathed first in a barn where I lay,
safe in the warmth of the sweet-smelling hay."

It was not the calf.

Someone was born this special day.
Was it you, little donkey?

The donkey snug in his coat of gray
shakes his head in a donkey way.

It was not the donkey.

Were you born this day, mourning dove?

"No, not I.
I was born in a nest of love
with leaves that whispered and sang above."

It was not the dove.

Is it your birthday, cedar tree?
"No, not mine.

When I was a seedling floating in space,
a wandering wind dropped me here in this place."

It was not the tree.

Was it you, little stone?
"No, not I.

I've been here since the world began
part of the great Creation plan."

It was not the stone.

Who was born this special day?

Was it the child?
The child who lies in the manger bed,
the shine of the star high overhead?

Clouds filled with angels shimmering bright,
singing of joy this dear, holy night.
Who was born this special day?

It was the child.